HORRID HENRY
AND THE
MEGA-MEAN
TIME
MACHINE

Meet HORRID HENRY
the laugh-out-loud
worldwide sensation!

....

★ Over 15 million copies sold in 27
  countries and counting

★ #1 chapter book series in the UK

★ Francesca Simon is the only American
  author to ever win the Galaxy British
  Book Awards Children's Book of the
  year (past winners include J.K. Rowling,
  Philip Pullman, and Eoin Colfer).

"Horrid Henry is a fabulous antihero...**a modern comic classic.**" —*Guardian*

"**Wonderfully appealing to girls and boys alike,** a precious rarity at this age." —Judith Woods, *Times*

"The best children's comic writer."
—Amanda Craig, *The Times*

"**I love the Horrid Henry books by Francesca Simon.** They have lots of funny bits in. And Henry always gets into trouble!" —Mia, age 6, *BBC Learning Is Fun*

"My two boys love this book, and **I have actually had tears running down my face and had to stop reading because of laughing so hard.**" —T. Franklin, Parent

"**It's easy to see why Horrid Henry is the bestselling character for five- to eight-year-olds.**" —*Liverpool Echo*

"Francesca Simon's truly horrific little boy is **a monstrously enjoyable creation.** Parents love them because Henry makes their own little darlings seem like angels." —*Guardian Children's Books Supplement*

"I have tried out the Horrid Henry books with groups of children as a parent, as a babysitter, and as a teacher. **Children love to either hear them read aloud or to read them themselves.**" —Danielle Hall, Teacher

"A flicker of recognition must pass through most teachers and parents when they read Horrid Henry. **There's a tiny bit of him in all of us.**" —Nancy Astee, *Child Education*

"**As a teacher...it's great to get a series of books my class loves.** They go mad for Horrid Henry." —A teacher

"**Henry is a beguiling hero who has entranced millions of reluctant readers.**" —*Herald*

....

"**An absolutely fantastic series and surely a winner with all children. Long live Francesca Simon and her brilliant books! More, more please!**"   —A parent

....

"**Laugh-out-loud reading for both adults and children alike.**" —A parent

"**Horrid Henry certainly lives up to his name, and his antics are everything you hope your own child will avoid—which is precisely why younger children so enjoy these tales.**"
—*Independent on Sunday*

"Henry might be unbelievably naughty, totally wicked, and utterly horrid, but **he is frequently credited with converting the most reluctant readers into enthusiastic ones**...superb in its simplicity." —*Liverpool Echo*

Horrid Henry by Francesca Simon

Horrid Henry

Horrid Henry Tricks the Tooth Fairy

Horrid Henry and the Mega-Mean Time Machine

Horrid Henry's Stinkbomb

Horrid Henry and the Mummy's Curse

Horrid Henry and the Soccer Fiend

HORRID HENRY
AND THE
MEGA-MEAN
TIME
MACHINE

Francesca Simon

Illustrated by Tony Ross

Published by Sourcebooks Jabberwocky, an imprint of Sourcebooks, Inc.
P.O. Box 4410, Naperville, Illinois 60567–4410
(630) 961–3900
Fax: (630) 961–2168
www.jabberwockykids.com

Originally published in Great Britain in 2005 by Orion Children's Books.

Library of Congress Cataloging-in-Publication Data

Simon, Francesca.
  Horrid Henry and the mega-mean time machine / Francesca Simon ; illus-
trated by Tony Ross.
     p. cm.
  Originally published: Great Britain : Orion Children's Books, 2005.
  [1. Behavior—Fiction.] I. Ross, Tony, ill. II. Title.
  PZ7.S604Hoam 2009
  [Fic]—dc22
                                    2008039687

                Printed and bound in the United States of America.
            VP 10 9 8 7 6 5 4 3 2 1

For my sister, Anne Simon, who reminded me about our time machine

CONTENTS

1   Horrid Henry's Hike   1

2   Horrid Henry and the
    Mega-Mean Time Machine   21

3   Perfect Peter's Revenge   41

4   Horrid Henry Dines
    at Restaurant Le Posh   67

1

HORRID HENRY'S HIKE

Horrid Henry looked out the window. AAARRRGGGHHH! It was a beautiful day. The sun was shining. The birds were tweeting. The breeze was blowing. Little fluffy clouds floated by in a bright blue sky.

Rats.

Why couldn't it be raining? Or hailing? Or sleeting?

Any minute, any second, it would happen…the words he'd been dreading, the words he'd give anything not to hear, the words—

"Henry! Peter! Time to go for a walk," called Mom.

"Yippee!" said Perfect Peter. "I can
wear my new yellow boots!"

"NO!" screamed Horrid Henry.

Go for a walk! Go for a walk! Didn't
he walk enough already? He walked to
school. He walked home from school.
He walked to the TV. He walked to
the computer. He walked to the candy
jar *and* all the way back to the comfy
black chair. Horrid Henry walked plenty.

Ugghh. The last thing he needed was
more walking. More chocolate, yes. More
chips, yes. More *walking?* No way! Why
oh why couldn't his parents ever say,

"Henry! Time to play on the computer."
Or "Henry, stop doing your homework
this minute! Time to turn on the TV."

But no. For some reason his mean,
horrible parents thought he spent too
much time sitting indoors. They'd been
threatening for weeks to make him go on a
family walk. Now the dreadful moment had
come. His precious weekend was ruined.

Horrid Henry hated nature. Horrid
Henry hated fresh air. What could be
more boring than walking up and down
streets staring at lampposts? Or sloshing
across some stupid muddy park? Nature
smelled. Uggh! He'd much rather be
inside watching TV.

Mom stomped into the living room.

"Henry! Didn't you hear me calling?"

"No," lied Henry.

"Get your boots on, we're going," said
Dad, rubbing his hands. "What a lovely
day."

"I don't want to go for a walk," said Henry. "I want to watch *Rapper Zapper Zaps Terminator Gladiator*."

"But Henry," said Perfect Peter, "fresh air and exercise are so good for you."

"I don't care!" shrieked Henry.

Horrid Henry stomped downstairs and flung open the front door. He breathed in deeply, hopped on one foot, then shut the door.

"There! Done it. Fresh air *and* exercise," snarled Henry.

"Henry, we're going," said Mom. "Get in the car."

Henry's ears pricked up.

"The car?" said Henry. "I thought we were going for a walk."

"We are," said Mom. "In the countryside."

"Hurray!" said Perfect Peter. "A nice *long* walk."

"NOOOO!" howled Henry. Plodding along in the boring old park was bad enough, with its moldy leaves and dog poo and stumpy trees. But at least the park wasn't very big. But the *countryside?*

The countryside was enormous! They'd be walking for hours, days, weeks, months, till his legs wore down to stumps and his feet fell off. And the countryside was so dangerous! Horrid Henry was sure he'd be swallowed up by quicksand or trampled to death by marauding chickens.

"I live in the city!" shrieked Henry. "I don't want to go to the country!"

"Time you got out more," said Dad.

"But look at those clouds," moaned

Henry, pointing to a fluffy wisp. "We'll get soaked."

"A little water never hurt anyone," said Mom.

Oh yeah? Wouldn't they be sorry when he died of pneumonia.

"I'm staying here and that's final!" screamed Henry.

"Henry, we're waiting," said Mom.

"Good," said Henry.

"*I'm* all ready, Mom," said Peter.

"I'm going to start deducting money from your allowance," said Dad. "Five cents, ten cents, fifteen cents, twenty—"

Horrid Henry pulled on his boots, stomped out the door, and got in the car. He slammed the door as hard as he could. It was so unfair! Why did he never get to do what *he* wanted to do? Now he would miss the first time Rapper Zapper had ever slugged it out with Terminator Gladiator. And all because he had to go on a long, boring, exhausting, horrible hike. He was so miserable he didn't even have the energy to kick Peter.

"Can't we just walk around the block?" moaned Henry.

"N-O spells no," said Dad. "We're going for a nice walk in the countryside and that's that."

Horrid Henry slumped miserably in his seat. Boy would they be sorry when he was gobbled up by goats. Boo hoo, if only we hadn't gone on that walk in the wild, Mom would wail.

Henry was right, we should have listened to

7

him, Dad would sob. I miss Henry, Peter would howl. I'll never eat goat's cheese again. And now it's too late, they would shriek.

If only, thought Horrid Henry. That would serve them right.

All too soon, Mom pulled into a parking lot, on the edge of a small forest.

"Wow," said Perfect Peter. "Look at all those pretty trees."

"Bet there are werewolves hiding there," muttered Henry. "And I hope they come and eat *you!*"

8

"Mom!" squealed Peter. "Henry's trying to scare me."

"Don't be horrid, Henry," said Mom.

Horrid Henry looked around him. There was a gate, leading to endless meadows bordered by bushes. A muddy path wound through the trees and across the fields. A church spire stuck up in the distance.

"All right, I've seen the countryside, let's go home," said Henry.

Mom glared at him.

"What?" said Henry, scowling.

"Let's enjoy this lovely day," said Dad, sighing.

"So what do we do now?" said Henry.

"Walk," said Dad.

"Where?" said Henry.

"Just walk," said Mom, "and enjoy the beautiful scenery."

Henry groaned.

"We're heading for the lake," said Dad, striding off. "I've brought bread and we can feed the ducks."

"But *Rapper Zapper* starts in an hour!"

"Tough," said Mom.

Mom, Dad, and Peter headed through the gate into the field. Horrid Henry trailed behind them walking as slowly as he could.

"Ahh, breathe the lovely fresh air," said Mom.

"We should do this more often," said Dad.

Henry sniffed.

The horrible smell of manure filled his nostrils.

"Ewww, smelly," said Henry. "Peter, couldn't you wait?"

"MOM!" shrieked Peter. "Henry called me smelly."

"Did not!"

"Did too!"

"Did not, smelly."

"WAAAAAAAAA!" wailed Peter. "Tell him to stop!"

"Don't be horrid, Henry!" screamed Mom. Her voice echoed. A dog walker passed her and glared.

"Peter, would you rather run a mile, jump a fence, or eat a country pancake?" said Henry sweetly.

"Ooh," said Peter. "I love pancakes.

And a country one must be even more delicious than a city one."

"Ha ha," cackled Horrid Henry, sticking out his tongue. "Fooled you. Peter wants to eat cow pies!"

"MOM!" screamed Peter.

Henry walked.

And walked.

And walked.

His legs felt heavier, and heavier, and heavier.

"This field is muddy," moaned Henry.

"I'm bored," groaned Henry.

"My feet hurt," complained Henry.

"Can't we go home? We've already walked miles," whined Henry.

"We've been walking for ten minutes," said Dad.

"Please can we go on walks more often," said Perfect Peter. "Oh, look at those fluffy little sheepies!"

Horrid Henry pounced. He was a zombie biting the head off the hapless human.

"AAAAEEEEEE!" squealed Peter.

"Henry!" screamed Mom.

"Stop it!" screamed Dad. "Or no TV for a week."

When he was king, thought Horrid Henry, any parent who made their children go on a hike would be dumped barefoot in a scorpion-infested desert.

Plod.

Plod.

Plod.

Horrid Henry dragged his feet. Maybe his horrible mean parents would get fed up waiting for him and turn back, he thought, kicking some moldy leaves.

Squelch.

Squelch.

Squelch.

Oh no, not *another* muddy meadow.

And then suddenly Horrid Henry had an idea. What was he thinking? All that fresh air must be rotting his brain. The sooner they got to the stupid lake, the sooner they could get home for *Rapper Zapper Zaps Terminator Gladiator.*

"Come on, everyone, let's run!" shrieked Henry. "Race you down the hill to the lake!"

"That's the spirit, Henry," said Dad.

 Horrid Henry dashed past Dad.

"OW!" shrieked Dad, tumbling into the stinging nettles.

Horrid Henry whizzed past Mom.

"Eww!" shrieked Mom, slipping in a cow pie.

Splat!

Horrid Henry pushed past Peter.

"Waaa!" wailed Peter. "My boots are getting dirty."

Horrid Henry scampered down the muddy path.

"Wait Henry!" yelped Mom. "It's too slipp—aaaiiieeeee!"

Mom slid down the path on her bottom.

"Slow down!" puffed Dad.

"I can't run that fast," wailed Peter.

But Horrid Henry raced on.

"Shortcut across the field!" he called. "Come on slowpokes!" The black and white cow grazing alone in the middle raised its head.

"Henry!" shouted Dad.

Horrid Henry kept running.

"I don't think that's a cow!" shouted Mom.

The cow lowered its head and charged.

"It's a bull!"

yelped Mom and Dad. "RUN!"

"I said it was dangerous in the countryside!" gasped Henry, as everyone clambered over the fence in the nick of time. "Look, there's the lake!" he added, pointing.

Henry ran down to the water's edge. Peter followed. The embankment narrowed to a point. Peter slipped past Henry and snagged the best spot, right at the water's edge where the ducks gathered.

"Hey, get away from there," said Henry.

"I want to feed the ducks," said Peter.

"I want to feed the ducks," said Henry. "Now move."

"I was here first," said Peter.

"Not any more," said Henry.

Horrid Henry pushed Peter.

"Out of my way, worm!"

Perfect Peter pushed him back.

"Don't call me worm!"

Henry wobbled.

Peter wobbled.

Splash!

Peter tumbled into the lake.

Crash!

Henry tumbled into the lake.

"My babies!" shrieked Mom, jumping in after them.

"My—glug glug glug!" shrieked Dad, jumping into the muddy water after her.

"My new boots!" gurgled Perfect Peter.

Bang!

Pow!

Terminator Gladiator slashed at Rapper Zapper.

Zap!

Rapper Zapper slashed back.

"Go Zappy!" yelled Henry, lying bundled up in blankets on the sofa. Once everyone had scrambled out of the lake, Mom and Dad wanted to get home as fast as possible.

"I think the park next time," mumbled Dad, sneezing.

"Definitely," mumbled Mom, coughing.

"Oh, I don't know," said Horrid Henry happily. "A little water never hurt anyone."

2

HORRID HENRY and THE MEGA-MEAN TIME MACHINE

Horrid Henry flicked the switch. The time machine whirred. Dials spun. Buttons pulsed. Latches locked. Horrid Henry Time Traveler was ready for blast-off!

Now, where to go, where to go?

Dinosaurs, thought Henry. Yes! Henry loved dinosaurs. He would love to stalk a few Tyrannosaurus Rexes as they rampaged through the primordial jungle.

But what about King Arthur and the Knights of the Round Table? "Arise, Sir Henry," King Arthur would say, kicking Lancelot out of his chair. "Sure thing, King," Sir Henry would reply, twirling his sword. "Out of my way, worms!"

Or what about the siege of Troy? Heroic Henry, that's who he'd be, the fearless fighter dashing about doing daring deeds.

Tempting, thought Henry. Very tempting.

Wait a sec, what about visiting the future, where school was banned and parents had to do whatever their children told them? Where everyone had their own spaceship and ate candy for dinner. And where King Henry the Horrible ruled supreme, chopping off the head of anyone who dared to say no to him.

To the future, thought Henry, setting the dial.

Bang! Pow!

Henry braced himself for the jolt into hyperspace—10, 9, 8, 7, 6—

"Henry, it's my turn."

Horrid Henry ignored the alien's whine. —5, 4, 3—

"Henry! If you don't share I'm going to tell Mom."

AAAARRRRGGGHHHHHH. The Time Machine shuddered to a halt. Henry climbed out.

"Go away, Peter," said Henry. "You're ruining everything."

"But it's my turn."

"GO AWAY!"

"Mom said we could *both* play with the

box," said Peter. "We could cut out windows, make a little house, paint flowers—"

"NO!" screeched Henry.

"But..." said Peter. He stood in the living room, holding his scissors and crayons.

"Don't you touch my box!" hissed Henry.

"I will if I want to," said Peter. "And it's not yours." Henry had no right to boss him around, thought Peter. He'd been waiting such a long time for his turn. Well, he wasn't waiting any longer. He'd start cutting out a window this minute.

Peter got out his scissors.

"Stop! It's a time machine, you toad!" shrieked Henry.

Peter paused.

Peter gasped.

Peter stared at the huge cardboard box. A time machine? *A time machine?* How could it be a time machine?

"It is not," said Peter.

24

"Is too," said Henry.

"But it's made of cardboard," said Peter. "And the washing machine came in it."

Henry sighed.

"Don't you know anything? If it *looked* like a time machine everyone would try to steal it. It's a time machine in *disguise*."

Peter looked at the time machine. On the one hand he didn't believe Henry for one minute. This was just one of Henry's tricks. Peter was a hundred million billion percent certain Henry was lying.

On the other hand, what if Henry *was* telling the truth for once and there was a real time machine in his living room?

"If it *is* a time machine, I want to have a turn," said Peter.

"You can't. You're too young," said Henry.

"Am not."

"Are too."

Perfect Peter stuck out his bottom lip.

"I don't believe you anyway."

Horrid Henry was outraged.

"Okay, I'll prove it. I'll go to the future right now. Stand back. Don't move."

Horrid Henry leaped into the box and closed the lid. The Time Machine began to shudder and shake.

Then everything was still for a very long time.

Perfect Peter didn't know what to do. What if Henry was gone—forever? What if he were stuck in the future?

I could have his room, thought Peter.

I could watch whatever I wanted on TV.
I could—

Suddenly the box tipped over and
Horrid Henry staggered out.

"Wh—wh—where am I?" he stut-
tered. Then he collapsed on the floor.

Peter stared at Henry.

Henry stared wildly at Peter.

"I've been to the future!" gasped
Henry, panting. "It was amazing.
Wow. I met my great-great-great-
grandson. He still lives in this house.
And he looks just like me."

"So he's ugly," muttered Peter.

"What—did—you—say?" hissed Henry.

"Nothing," said Peter quickly. He
didn't know what to think. "Is this a
trick, Henry?"

"Course it isn't," said Henry. "And just
for that I won't let you have a turn."

"I can if I want to," said Peter.

"You keep away from my time machine,"

said Henry. "One wrong move and you'll get blasted into the future."

Perfect Peter walked a few steps toward the time machine. Then he paused.

"What's it like in the future?"

"Boys wear dresses," said Horrid Henry. "And lipstick. People talk Ugg language. *You'd* probably like it. Everyone just eats vegetables."

"Really?"

"And kids have tons of homework."

Perfect Peter loved homework.

"Ooohh." This Peter *had* to see. Just in case Henry *was* telling the truth.

"I'm going to the future and you can't stop me," said Peter.

"Go ahead," said Henry. Then he snorted. "You can't go looking like that!"

"Why not?" said Peter.

"'Cause everyone will laugh at you."

Perfect Peter hated people laughing at him.

"Why?"

"Because to them you'll look weird. Are you sure you really want to go to the future?"

"Yes," said Peter.

"Are you sure you're sure?"

"YES," said Peter.

"Then I'll get you ready," said Henry solemnly.

"Thank you, Henry," said Peter. Maybe he'd been wrong about Henry. Maybe going to the future had turned him into a nice brother.

Horrid Henry dashed out of the living room.

Perfect Peter felt a quiver of excitement. The future. What if Henry really was telling the truth?

Horrid Henry returned carrying a large wicker basket. He pulled out an old red dress of Mom's, some lipstick, and a black frothy drink.

"Here, put this on," said Henry.

Perfect Peter put on the dress. It dragged onto the floor.

"Now, with a bit of lipstick," said Horrid Henry, applying big blobs of red lipstick all over Peter's face, "you'll fit right in. Perfect," he said, standing back to admire his handiwork. "You look just like a boy from the future."

"Okay," said Perfect Peter.

"Now listen carefully," said Henry. "When you arrive, you won't be able to speak the language unless you drink this bibble babble drink. Take this with you and drink it when you get there."

Henry held out the frothy black drink from his Dungeon Drink Kit. Peter took it.

"You can now enter the time machine." Peter obeyed. His heart was pounding.

"Don't get out until the time machine has stopped moving completely. Then count to twenty-five, and open the hatch very very slowly. You don't want a piece of you in the twenty-third century, and the rest here in the twenty-first. Good luck."

Henry swirled the box around and around and around. Peter began to feel dizzy. The drink sloshed on the floor.

Then everything was still.

Peter's head was spinning. He counted to twenty-five, then crept out.

He was in the living room of a house that looked just like his. A boy wearing a bathrobe and silver waggly antennae with his face painted in blue stripes stood in front of him.

"Ugg?" said the strange boy.

"Henry?" said Peter.

"Uggg uggg bleuch ble bloop," said the boy.

"Uggg uggg," said Peter uncertainly.

"Uggh uggh drink ugggh," said the boy, pointing to Peter's bibble babble drink.

Peter drank the few drops which were left.

"I'm Zog," said Zog. "Who are you?"

"I'm Peter," said Peter.

"Ahhhhh! Welcome! You must be my great-great-great-uncle Peter. Your very nice brother Henry told me all about you when he visited me from the past."

"Oh, what did he say?" said Peter.

"That you were an ugly toad."

"I am not," said Peter. "Wait a minute," he added suspiciously. "Henry said that boys wore dresses in the future."

"They do," said Zog quickly. "I'm a girl."

"Oh," said Peter. He gasped. Henry

would *never* in a million years say he was a girl. Not even if he were being poked with red hot pokers. Could it be...

Peter looked around. "This looks just like my living room."

Zog snorted.

"Of course it does, Uncle Pete. This is now the Peter Museum. You're famous in the future. Everything has been kept exactly as it was."

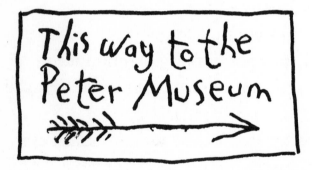

Peter beamed. He was famous in the future. He always knew he'd be famous. A Peter Museum! He couldn't wait to tell Spotless Sam and Tidy Ted.

There was just one more thing...

"What about Henry?" he asked. "Is he famous too?"

"Nah," said Zog smoothly. "He's known as What's-His-Name, Peter's older brother."

Ahh. Peter swelled with pride. Henry was in his lowly place, at last. That proved it. He'd really traveled to the future!

Peter looked out the window. Strange how the future didn't look so different from his own time.

Zog pointed.

"Our spaceships," he announced.

Peter stared. Spaceships looked just like cars.

"Why aren't they flying?" said Peter.

"Only at nighttime," said Zog. "You can either drive 'em or fly 'em."

"Wow," said Peter.

"Don't *you* have spaceships?" said Zog.

"No," said Peter. "Cars."

"I didn't know they had cars in olden

days," said Zog. "Do you have blitzkatrons
and zappersnappers?"

"No," said Peter. "What—"

The front door slammed. Mom walked
in. She stared at Peter.

"What on earth..."

"Don't be scared," said Peter. "I'm
Peter. I come from the past. I'm your
great-great-great grandfather."

Mom looked at Peter.

Peter looked at Mom.

"Why are you wearing my dress?" said
Mom.

"It's not one of *yours*, silly," said Peter.
"It belonged to my mom."

"I see," said Mom.

"Come on, Uncle Pete," said Zog quickly, taking Peter firmly by the arm, "I'll show you our supersonic hammock in the back yard."

"Okay, Zog," said Peter happily.

Mom beamed.

"It's so wonderful to see you playing nicely with your brother, Henry."

Perfect Peter stood still.

"What did you call him?"

"Henry," said Mom.

Peter felt a chill.

"So his name's not Zog? And he's not a girl?"

"Not the last time I looked," said Mom.

"And this house isn't...the Peter Museum?"

Mom glared at Henry. "Henry! Have you been teasing Peter again?"

"Ha ha tricked you!" shrieked Henry. "Na Na Ne Nah Nah, wait till I tell everybody!"

"NO!" squealed Peter. "NOOOOOOO!"
How *could* he have believed his horrible
brother?

"Henry! You horrid boy! Go to your
room! No TV for the rest of the day,"
said Mom.

But Horrid Henry didn't care. The
Mega-Mean Time Machine would go
down in history as his greatest trick ever.

3

PERFECT PETER'S REVENGE

Perfect Peter had had enough. Why oh why did he always fall for Henry's tricks?

Every time it happened he swore Henry would never ever trick him again. And every time he fell for it. How *could* he have believed that there were fairies at the bottom of the garden? Or that there was such a thing as a Fangmangler? But the time machine was the worst. The very very worst. Everyone had teased him. Even Goody-Goody Gordon asked him if he'd seen any spaceships recently.

Well, never again. His mean, horrible brother had tricked him for the very last time.

I'll get my revenge, thought Perfect Peter, pasting the last of his animal stamps into his album. I'll make Henry sorry for being so mean to me.

But what horrid mean nasty thing could he do? Peter had never tried to take revenge on anyone.

He asked Tidy Ted.

"Mess up his room," said Ted.

But Henry's room was already a mess.

He asked Spotless Sam.

"Put a spaghetti stain on his shirt," said Sam.

But Henry's shirts were already stained.

Peter picked up a copy of his favorite magazine *Best Boy*. Maybe it would have some handy hints on the perfect revenge. He searched the table of contents:

- IS <u>YOUR</u> BEDROOM AS TIDY AS IT COULD BE?
- TEN TOP TIPS FOR PLEASING YOUR PARENTS
- HOW TO POLISH YOUR TROPHIES

- WHY MAKING YOUR BED IS GOOD FOR YOU
- READERS TELL US ABOUT THEIR FAVORITE CHORES!

Reluctantly, Peter closed *Best Boy* magazine. Somehow he didn't think he'd find the answer inside. He was on his own.

I'll tell Mom that Henry eats candy in his bedroom, thought Peter. Then Henry would get into trouble. Big big trouble.

But Henry got into trouble all the time. That wouldn't be anything special.

I know, thought Peter, I'll hide Mr. Kill. Henry would never admit it, but he couldn't sleep without Mr. Kill. But so what if Henry couldn't sleep? He'd just come and jump on Peter's head or sneak downstairs and watch scary movies.

I have to think of something really, really horrid, thought Peter. It was hard for Peter to think horrid thoughts, but Peter was determined to try.

43

He would call Henry a horrid name, like Ugly Toad or Poo Poo Face. *That* would show him.

But if I did, Henry would hit me, thought Peter.

Wait, he could tell everyone at school that Henry wore diapers. Henry the big diaper. Henry the big smelly diaper. Henry diaper face. Henry poopy pants. Peter smiled happily. That would be the perfect revenge.

Then he stopped smiling. Sadly, no one at school would believe that Henry still wore diapers. Worse, they might think that Peter still did! Eeeek.

I've got it, thought Peter, I'll put a muddy twig in Henry's bed. Peter had

44

read a great story about a younger brother who'd done just that to a mean older one. That would serve Henry right.

But was a muddy twig enough revenge for all of Henry's crimes against him?

No it was not.

I give up, thought Peter, sighing. It was hopeless. He just couldn't think of anything horrid enough.

Peter sat down on his beautifully made bed and opened *Best Boy* magazine.

TELL MOM HOW MUCH YOU LOVE HER!

shrieked the headline.

And then a dreadful thought tiptoed

into his head. It was so dreadful, and so horrid, that Perfect Peter could not believe that he had thought it.

"No," he gasped. "I couldn't." That was too evil.

But...but...wasn't that exactly what he wanted? A horrid revenge on a horrid brother?

"Don't do it!" begged his angel.

"Do it!" urged his devil, thrilled to

get the chance to speak. "Go on, Peter! Henry deserves it."

YES! thought Peter. He would do it. He would have revenge!

Perfect Peter sat down at the computer. Tap tap tap.

Dear Margaret,
I love you. Will you marry me?

Peter printed out the note and carefully scrawled:

HENrY

There! thought Peter proudly. That looks just like Henry's writing. He folded the note, then sneaked into the garden, climbed over the wall, and left it on the

table inside Moody Margaret's Secret
Club tent.

"Of course Henry loves me," said Moody
Margaret, primping. "He can't help it.
Everyone loves me because I'm so lovable."

"No you're not," said Sour Susan.
"You're moody. And you're mean."
"Am not!"

"Are too!"

"Am not. You're just jealous 'cause no one would *ever* want to marry you," snapped Margaret.

"I am not jealous. Anyway, Henry likes *me* the best," said Susan, waving a folded piece of paper.

"Says who?"

"Says Henry."

Margaret snatched the paper from Susan's hand and read:

TO THE BEAUTIFUL SUSAN

Oh Susan,
No one is as pretty as you,
you always smell lovely
Just like shampoo.
HENry

Margaret sniffed. "Just like dog poo, you mean."

"I do not," shrieked Susan.

"Is this your idea of a joke?" snorted Moody Margaret, crumpling the poem.

Sour Susan was outraged.

"No. It was waiting for me on the clubhouse table. You're just jealous because Henry didn't write *you* a poem."

"Huh," said Margaret. Well, she'd show Henry. No one made a fool of her.

Margaret snatched up a pen and scribbled a reply to Henry's note.

"Take this to Henry and report straight back," she ordered. "I'll wait here for Linda and Gurinder."

"Take it yourself," said Susan sourly. Why oh why was she friends with such a mean, moody, jealous grump?

Horrid Henry was inside the Purple Hand Fort plotting death to the Secret Club and scarfing down cookies when an enemy agent peered through the entrance.

"Guard!" shrieked Henry.

But that miserable worm toad was nowhere to be found.

Henry reminded himself to fire Peter immediately.

"Halt! Who goes there?"

"I have an important message," said the Enemy.

"Make it snappy," said Henry. "I'm busy."

Susan crept beneath the branches.

"Do you really like my shampoo, Henry?" she asked.

Henry stared at Susan. She had a sick smile on her face, as if her stomach hurt.

"Huh?" said Henry.

"You know, my *shampoo*," said Susan, simpering.

Had Susan finally gone crazy?

"*That's* your message?" said Horrid Henry.

"No," said Susan, scowling. She tossed a scrunched-up piece of paper at Henry and marched off.

Henry opened the note:

I wouldn't marry you if you were the last creature on earth and that includes slimy toads and rattlesnakes. So there.

Margaret

Henry choked on his cookie. Marry Margaret?! He'd rather walk around town carrying a Walkie-Talkie-Burpy-Slurpy-Teasy-Weasy Doll. He'd rather learn long division. He'd rather trade all his computer games for a Princess Pamper Parlor. He'd rather...he'd rather...he'd rather marry Miss Battle-Axe than marry Margaret!

What on earth had given Margaret the crazy, horrible, revolting idea he wanted to marry *her?*

He always knew Margaret was nuts. Now he had proof. Well well well, thought Horrid Henry gleefully. Wouldn't he tease her! Margaret would never live this down.

Henry leaped over the wall and burst into the Secret Club Tent.

"Margaret, you old pants face, I wouldn't marry you if—"

"Henry loves Margaret! Henry loves Margaret!" chanted Gorgeous Gurinder.

"Henry loves Margaret! Henry loves Margaret!" chanted Lazy Linda, making horrible kissing sounds.

Henry tried to speak. He opened his mouth. Then he closed it.

"No I don't," gasped Horrid Henry.

"Oh yeah?" said Gurinder.

"Yeah," said Henry.

"Then why'd you send her a note saying you did?"

"I didn't!" howled Henry.

"And you sent Susan a poem!" said Linda.

"I DID NOT!" howled Henry even louder. What on earth was going on? He took a step backward.

The Secret Club members advanced on him, shrieking, "Henry loves Margaret, Henry loves Margaret."

Time, thought Horrid Henry, to make a strategic retreat. He dashed back to his fort, the terrible words "Henry loves Margaret" burning his ears.

"PETER!" bellowed Horrid Henry. "Come here this minute!"

Perfect Peter crept out of the house to the fort. Henry had found out about the note and the poem. He was dead.

Good-bye, cruel world, thought Peter.

"Did you see anyone going into the Secret Club carrying a note?" demanded Henry, glaring.

Perfect Peter's heart began to beat again.

"No," said Peter. That wasn't a lie because he hadn't seen himself.

"I want you to stand guard by the wall, and report anyone suspicious to me at once," said Henry.

"Why?" said Peter innocently.

"None of your business, worm," snapped Henry. "Just do as you're told."

"Yes, Lord High Excellent Majesty of the Purple Hand," said Perfect Peter. What a lucky escape!

Henry sat on his Purple Hand throne and thought. Who was this foul fiend? Who was this evil genius? Who was spreading these nasty rumors? He had to find out, then strike back hard before the snake struck again.

But who'd want to be his enemy? He was such a nice, kind, friendly boy.

True, Rude Ralph wasn't very happy when Henry called him Ralphie Walfie.

Tough Toby wasn't too pleased when Henry depantsed him during playtime.

And for some reason, Brainy Brian didn't see the joke when Henry scribbled all over his book report.

Vain Violet said she'd pay Henry back for pulling her pigtails.

And just the other day Fiery Fiona said Henry would be sorry he'd laughed during her speech in the assembly.

Even Kind Kasim warned Henry to stop being so horrid or he'd teach him a lesson he wouldn't forget.

But maybe Margaret was behind the whole plot. He had stinkbombed her Secret Club, after all.

Hmmm. The list of suspects was rather long.

It had to be Ralph. Ralph loved playing practical jokes.

Well, it's not funny, Ralph, thought Horrid Henry. Let's see how *you* like it. Perhaps a little poem to Miss Battle-Axe...

Horrid Henry grabbed a piece of paper and began to scribble:

Oh Boudicca dear,
Whenever you're near,
I just want to cheer,
Oh big old teacher
Your carrot nose is your best feature
You are so sweet
I would like to kiss your feet
What a treat
Even though they smell of meat
Dear Miss Battle-Axe
Clear out your earwax
So you can hear me say...
No need to frown
But your pants are falling down!

Ha ha ha ha ha,
thought Henry.
He'd sign the
poem "Ralph,"
get to school early,
and pin the poem

on the door of the girls' bathroom.
Ralph would get into big big trouble.

But wait.

What if Ralph *wasn't* responsible?

Could it be Toby after all? Or Margaret?

There was only one thing to do.
Henry copied his poem seven times,
signing each copy with a different name.
He would post them all over school
tomorrow. One of them was sure to
be guilty.

Henry sneaked into school, then quickly
pinned up his poems on every bulletin
board. That done, he swaggered onto the

playground. Revenge is sweet, thought Horrid Henry.

There was a crowd gathered outside the boys' bathroom.

"What's going on?" shrieked Horrid Henry, pushing and shoving his way through the crowd.

"Henry loves Margaret," chanted Tough Toby.

"Henry loves Margaret," chanted Rude Ralph.

Uh oh.

Henry glanced at the bathroom door. There was a note taped on it.

Dear Margaret,
I love you. Will you marry me?
HENry

Henry's blood froze. He ripped the note off the door.

"Margaret wrote it to herself," blustered Horrid Henry.

"Didn't!" said Margaret.

"Did!" said Henry.

"Besides, you love *me!*" shrieked Susan.

"No I don't!" shrieked Henry.

"That's 'cause you love me!" said Margaret.

"I hate you!" shouted Henry.

"I hate you more!" said Margaret.

"I hate *you* more," said Henry.

"You started it," said Margaret.

"Didn't."

"Did! You asked me to marry you."

"NO WAY!" shrieked Henry.

"And you sent me a poem!" said Susan.

"No I didn't!" howled Henry.

"Well, if you didn't then who did?" said Margaret.

Silence.

"Henry," came a little voice, "can we play pirates after school today?"

Horrid Henry thought an incredible thought.

Moody Margaret thought an incredible thought.

Sour Susan thought an incredible thought.

Three pairs of eyes stared at Perfect Peter.

"Wha...what?" said Peter.

Uh oh.

"HELP!" shrieked Perfect Peter. He turned and ran.

"AAAARRRRRGHHHHHH!" shrieked Horrid Henry, chasing after him. "You're dead meat, worm!"

Miss Battle-Axe marched onto the playground. She was clutching a sheaf of papers in her hand.

"Margaret! Brian! Ralph! Toby! Violet! Kasim! Fiona! What is the meaning of these poems? Straight to the principal's office— now!" Perfect Peter crashed into her.

Smash!

Miss Battle-Axe toppled backward into the garbage.

"And you too, Peter," gasped Miss Battle-Axe.

"Waaaaaaa!" wailed Perfect Peter. From now on, he'd definitely be sticking to good deeds. Whoever said revenge was sweet didn't have a horrid brother like Henry.

4

HORRID HENRY DINES AT RESTAURANT LE POSH

"Great news, everyone," said Mom, beaming. "Aunt Ruby is taking us all out for dinner to Le Posh, the best French restaurant in town."

"Oh boy, Restaurant Le Posh," said Perfect Peter. "We've never been there."

Horrid Henry stopped scribbling all over Peter's stamp album. His heart sank. French? Restaurant? Oh no. That meant strange, horrible, yucky food. That meant no burgers, no ketchup, no pizza. That meant—

"NOOOOOOOOOOO! I don't want to go there!" howled Henry. Who knew what revolting poison would arrive on his plate, covered in gloopy sauce with green pieces floating around. Uggghh.

"It's Mom's birthday," said Dad, "so we're celebrating."

"I only like Whopper Whoopee," said Henry. "Or Fat Frank's. I don't want to go to Le Posh."

"But Henry," said Perfect Peter, tidying up his toys, "it's a chance to try new food."

Mom beamed. "Exactly, Peter. It's always nice to try new things."

"No it isn't," snarled Horrid Henry. "I hate trying new food when there's nothing wrong with the old."

"I love it," said Dad. "I eat everything except tomatoes."

"And I eat everything except squid," said Mom.

"And I love all vegetables except beets," said Perfect Peter. "Especially spinach and sprouts."

"Well I don't," shrieked Horrid Henry. "Do they have pasta?"

"Whatever they have will be delicious," said Mom firmly.

"Do they have burgers? If they don't I'm not going," wailed Horrid Henry.

Mom looked at Dad.

Dad looked at Mom.

Last time they'd taken Henry to a fancy restaurant he'd had a tantrum under the table. The time before he'd run screaming around the room snatching all the salt and pepper shakers and then threw up on the people at the next table. The time before that—Mom and Dad preferred not to think about that.

"Should we get a babysitter?" murmured Dad.

"Leave him home on my birthday?" murmured Mom. She allowed herself to be tempted for a moment. Then she sighed.

"Henry, you are coming and you will be on your best behavior," said Mom. "Your cousin Steve will be there. You wouldn't want Steve to see you make a fuss, would you?"

The hairs on the back of Henry's neck stood up. Steve! Stuck-Up Steve! Horrid Henry's archenemy and the world's worst cousin. If there was a slimier boy than

 Steve slithering around then Horrid Henry would eat worms.

Last time they'd met Henry had tricked Steve into thinking there was a monster

under his bed. Steve had sworn revenge. There was nothing Steve wouldn't do to get back at Henry.

Boy, did Horrid Henry hate Stuck-Up Steve.

Boy, did Stuck-Up Steve hate Horrid Henry.

"I'm not coming and that's final!" screamed Horrid Henry.

"Henry," said Dad. "I'll make a deal with you."

"What deal?" said Henry. It was always wise to be suspicious when parents offered deals.

"I want you to be pleasant and talk to everyone. And you will eat everything on your plate like everyone else without making a fuss. If you do, I'll give you $2."

Two dollars! Two whole dollars! Horrid Henry gasped. Two whole dollars just for talking and shoving a few

mouthfuls of
disgusting
food
in his
mouth.

Normally he had to do that for free.

"How about $3?" said Henry.

"Henry..." said Mom.

"OK, deal," said Horrid Henry. But I won't eat a thing and they can't make me, he thought. He'd find a way. Dad said he had to eat everything on his plate. Well, maybe some food wouldn't *stay* on his plate...Horrid Henry smiled.

Perfect Peter stopped putting away his blocks. He frowned. Shouldn't *he* get two dollars like Henry?

"What's *my* reward for being good?" said Perfect Peter.

"Goodness is its own reward," said Dad.

★ ★ ★

The restaurant was hushed. The tables were covered in snowy-white table-cloths, with yellow silk chairs. Huge gold chandeliers dangled from the ceiling. Crystal glasses twinkled. The rectangular china plates sparkled. Horrid Henry was impressed.

"Wow," said Henry. It was like walking into a palace.

"Haven't you ever been here before?" sneered Stuck-Up Steve.

"No," said Henry.

"*We* eat here all the time," said Steve. "I guess you're too poor."

"It's 'cause *we'd* rather eat at Whopper Whoopee," lied Henry.

"Hush, Steve," said Rich Aunt Ruby. "I'm sure Whopper Whoopee is a lovely restaurant."

Steve snorted.

Henry kicked him under the table.

"OWWWW!" yelped Steve. "Henry kicked me!"

"No I didn't," said Henry. "It was an accident."

"Henry," said Mom through gritted teeth. "Remember what we said about best behavior? We're in a fancy restaurant."

Horrid Henry scowled. He looked cautiously around. It was just as he'd feared. Everyone was busy eating weird

pieces of this and that, covered in gloopy
sauces. Henry checked under the tables
to see if anyone was throwing up yet.

There was no one lying poisoned under
the tables. I guess it's just a matter of time,
thought Henry grimly. You won't catch
me eating anything here.

Mom, Dad, Peter and Rich Aunt
Ruby blabbed away at their end of the
table. Horrid Henry sat sullenly next to
Stuck-Up Steve.

"I've got a new bike," Steve bragged. "Do you still have that old rust bucket you had last Christmas?"

"Hush, Steve," said Rich Aunt Ruby.

Horrid Henry's foot got ready to kick Steve.

"Boudicca Battle-Axe! How many times have I told you—don't chew with your mouth open," boomed a terrible voice.

Horrid Henry looked up. His jaw dropped.

There was his terrifying teacher, Miss Battle-Axe, sitting at a small table in the corner with her back to him. She was

with someone even taller, skinnier, and more ferocious than she was.

"And take your elbows off the table!"

"Yes, Mom," said Miss Battle-Axe meekly.

Henry could not believe his ears. Did teachers have mothers? Did teachers ever leave the school? Impossible.

"Boudicca! Stop slouching!"

"Yes, Mom," said Miss Battle-Axe, straightening up a fraction.

"So, what's everyone having?" beamed Aunt Ruby. Horrid Henry tore his eyes away from Miss Battle-Axe and stared

at the menu. It was entirely written in French.

"I recommend the mussels," said Aunt Ruby.

"Mussels! Ick!" shrieked Henry.

"Or the blah blah blah blah blah." Aunt Ruby pronounced a few mysterious French words.

"Maybe," said Mom. She looked a little uncertain.

"Maybe," said Dad. He looked a little uncertain.

"You order for me, Aunt Ruby," said Perfect Peter. "I eat everything."

Horrid Henry had no idea what food Aunt Ruby had suggested, but he knew he hated every single thing on the menu.

"I want a burger," said Henry.

"No burgers here," said Mom firmly. "This is Restaurant Le Posh."

"I said I want a burger!" shouted Henry. Several diners looked up.

"Don't be horrid, Henry!" hissed Mom.

"I CAN'T UNDERSTAND THIS MENU!" screamed Henry.

"Calm down this minute Henry," hissed Dad. "Or no $2."

Mom translated: "A tasty...uh...something on a bed of roast something with a something sauce."

"Sounds delicious," said Dad.

"Wait, there's more," said Mom. "A big piece of something enrobed with something cooked in something with carrots."

"Right, I'm having that," said Dad. "I love carrots."

Mom carried on translating. Henry opened his mouth to scream—

"Why don't you order *tripe?*" said Steve.

"What's that?" asked Henry suspiciously.

"You don't want to know," said Steve.

"Try me," said Henry.

"Intestines," said Steve. "You know, the wriggly bits in your stomach."

Horrid Henry snorted. Sometimes he felt sorry for Steve. Did Steve really think he'd fool him with *that* old trick? *Tripe* was probably a fancy French word for spaghetti. Or cake.

"Or you could order *escargots*," said Steve. "I dare you."

"What's *escargots?*" said Henry.

Stuck-Up Steve stuck his nose in the air.

"Oh, sorry, I forgot you don't learn French at your school. *I've* been learning it for years."

"Whoopee for you," said Horrid Henry.

"*Escargots* are snails, stupid," said Stuck-Up Steve.

Steve must think he was a real idiot, thought Horrid Henry indignantly. *Snails*. Ha ha ha. In a restaurant? As if.

"Oh yeah, right, you big fat liar," said Henry.

Steve shrugged.

"Too chicken, huh?" he sneered. "Cluck cluck cluck."

Horrid Henry was outraged. No one called him chicken and lived.

"Course not," said Horrid Henry. "I'd love to eat snails." Naturally it would turn out to be fish or something in a smelly, disgusting sauce, but so what? *Escargots* could hardly be more revolting than all the other yucky things on the menu. Steve would have to try harder than that to fool him. He would order so-called "snails" just to show Steve up for the liar he was. Then wouldn't he make fun of stupid old Steve!

"And vat are ve having tonight?" asked the French waiter.

Aunt Ruby ordered.

"An excellent choice, madame," said the waiter.

Dad ordered. The waiter kissed his fingers.

"*Magnifique*, monsieur, our speciality."

Mom ordered.

"Bravo, madame. And what about you, young man?" the waiter asked Henry.

"I'm having *escargots*," said Henry.

"Hmmm," said the waiter. "Monsieur is a gourmet?"

Horrid Henry wasn't sure he liked the sound of that. Stuck-Up Steve snickered. What was going on? thought Horrid Henry.

"Boudicca! Eat your vegetables!"

"Yes, Mom."

"Boudicca! Stop slurping."

"Yes, Mom," snapped Miss Battle-Axe.

"Boudicca! Don't pick your nose!"

"I wasn't!" said Miss Battle-Axe.

"Don't you contradict me," said Mrs. Battle-Axe.

The waiter reappeared, carrying six plates covered in silver domes.

"Voilà!" he said, whisking off the lids with a flourish. "Bon appétit!"

Everyone peered at their elegant plates.

"Ah," said Mom, looking at her squid.

"Ah," said Dad, looking at his stuffed tomatoes.

"Ah," said Peter, looking at his beet mousse.

Horrid Henry stared at his food. It looked like—it couldn't be—oh my gosh, it was...SNAILS! It really was snails! Squishy squashy squidgy slimy slithery slippery snails. Still in their shells. Drenched in butter, but unmistakably snails. Steve had tricked him.

Horrid Henry's hand reached out to hurl the snails at Steve.

Stuck-Up Steve giggled.

Horrid Henry stopped and gritted his teeth. No way was he giving Steve the satisfaction of seeing him get into big trouble. He'd ordered snails and he'd eat snails. And when he threw up, he'd make sure it was all over Steve.

Horrid Henry grabbed his fork and plunged. Then he closed his eyes and popped the snail in his mouth.

Horrid Henry chewed.

Horrid Henry chewed some more.

"Hmmm," said Horrid Henry.

He popped another snail in his mouth. And another.

"Yummy," said Henry. "This is great." Why hadn't anyone told him that Le Posh served such thrillingly revolting food? Wait till he told Rude Ralph!

Stuck-Up Steve looked unhappy.

"How's your maggot sauce, Steve?" said Henry cheerfully.

"It's not maggot sauce," said Steve.

"Maggot maggot maggot," whispered Henry. "Watch them wriggle about."

Steve put down his fork. So did Mom, Dad, and Peter.

"Go on everyone, eat up," said Henry, chomping.

"I'm not that hungry," said Mom.

"You said we had to eat everything on our plate," said Henry.

"No I didn't," said Dad weakly.

"You did too!" said Henry. "So eat!"

"I don't like beets," moaned Perfect Peter.

"Hush, Peter," snapped Mom.

"Peter, I never thought *you* were a fussy eater," said Aunt Ruby.

"I'm not!" wailed Perfect Peter.

"Boudicca!" blasted Mrs. Battle-Axe's shrill voice. "Pay attention when I'm speaking to you!"

"Yes, Mom," said Miss Battle-Axe.

"Why can't you be as good as that boy?" said Mrs. Battle-Axe, pointing to Horrid Henry. "Look at him sitting there, eating so beautifully."

Miss Battle-Axe turned around and saw Henry. Her face went bright red, then

purple, then white. She gave him a sickly
smile.

Horrid Henry gave her a little polite
wave. Oh boy.

For the first time in his life was he ever
looking forward to school.

And now for a sneak peek at one of the laugh-out-loud
stories in *Horrid Henry's Stinkbomb*

HORRID HENRY'S
STINKBOMB

"I hate you, Margaret!" shrieked Sour
Susan. She stumbled out of the Secret
Club tent.

"I hate you too!" shrieked Moody
Margaret.

Sour Susan stuck out her tongue.

Moody Margaret stuck out hers back.

"I quit!" yelled Susan.

"You can't quit. You're fired!" yelled
Margaret.

"You can't fire me. I quit!" said Susan.

"I fired you first," said Margaret. "And
I'm changing the password!"

"Go ahead. See if I care. I don't want

to be in the Secret Club any more!"
said Susan sourly.

"Good! Because *we* don't want you."

Moody Margaret flounced back inside the Secret Club tent. Sour Susan stalked off.

Free at last! Susan was sick and tired of her ex-best friend Bossyboots Margaret. Blaming *her* for the disastrous raid on the Purple Hand Fort when it was all Margaret's fault was bad enough. But then to ask stupid Linda to join the Secret Club without even telling her! Susan hated Linda even more than she hated Margaret. Linda hadn't invited Susan to her sleepover party. And she was a copycat. But Margaret didn't care. Today she'd made Linda chief spy. Well, Susan had had enough. Margaret had been mean to her once too often.

Susan heard roars of laughter from inside the club tent. So they were laughing, were they? Laughing at her, no doubt? Well, she'd show them. She knew all about Margaret's Top Secret Plans. And she knew someone who would be very interested in that information.

"Halt! Password!"

"Smelly toads," said Perfect Peter. He waited outside Henry's Purple Hand Fort.

"Wrong," said Horrid Henry.

"What's the new one then?" said Perfect Peter.

"I'm not telling *you*," said Henry. "You're fired, remember?"

Perfect Peter did remember. He had hoped Henry had forgotten.

"Can't I join again, Henry?" asked Peter.

"No way!" said Horrid Henry.

"Please?" said Perfect Peter.

"No," said Horrid Henry. "Ralph's taken over your duties."

Rude Ralph poked his head through the branches of Henry's lair.

"No babies allowed," said Rude Ralph.

"We don't want you here, Peter," said Horrid Henry. "Get lost."

Perfect Peter burst into tears.

"Crybaby!" jeered Horrid Henry.

"Crybaby!" jeered Rude Ralph.

That did it.

"Mom!" wailed Perfect Peter. He ran toward the house. "Henry won't let me play and he called me a crybaby!"

"Stop being horrid, Henry!" shouted Mom.

Peter waited.

Mom didn't say anything else.

Perfect Peter started to wail louder.

"Mooom! Henry's being mean to me!"

"Leave Peter alone, Henry!" shouted Mom. She came out of the house. Her hands were covered in dough. "Henry, if you don't stop—"

Mom looked around.

"Where's Henry?"

"In his fort," sniveled Peter.

"I thought you said he was being mean to you," said Mom.

"He was!" wailed Peter.

"Just keep away from him," said Mom. She went back into the house.

Perfect Peter was out-raged. Was that it? Why hadn't she punished Henry? Henry had been so horrid he deserved to go to prison for a year. Two years. And just get a crust of bread a week. And brussels sprouts. Ha! That would serve Henry right.

But until Henry went to prison, how could Peter pay him back?

And then Peter knew exactly what he could do.

He checked carefully to see that no one was watching. Then he sneaked over the garden wall and headed for the Secret Club Tent.

....

Will Peter tell Margaret all of Henry's Purple Hand plans? Will Susan sabotage Margaret's Secret Club attack on Henry? Find out whose fort is still standing at the end of the battle in *Horrid Henry's Stinkbomb*.

HORRID HENRY

Henry is dragged to dancing class against his will; vies with Moody Margaret to make the yuckiest Glop; goes camping; and tries to be good like Perfect Peter—but not for long.

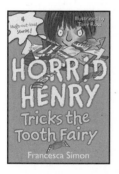

HORRID HENRY TRICKS THE TOOTH FAIRY

Horrid Henry tries to trick the Tooth Fairy into giving him more money; sends Moody Margaret packing; causes his teachers to run screaming from school; and single-handedly wrecks a wedding.

HORRID HENRY'S STINKBOMB

Horrid Henry uses a stinkbomb as a toxic weapon in his long-running war with Moody Margaret; uses all his tricks to win the school reading competition; goes for a sleepover and retreats in horror when he finds that other people's houses aren't always as nice as his own; and has the joy of seeing Miss Battle-Axe in hot water with the principle when he knows it was all his fault.

HORRID HENRY
AND THE
MUMMY'S CURSE

Horrid Henry indulges his favorite hobby—collecting Gizmos; has a bad time with his spelling homework; starts a rumor that there's a shark in the pool; and spooks Perfect Peter with the mummy's curse.

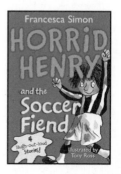

HORRID HENRY
AND THE
SOCCER FIEND

Horrid Henry reads Perfect Peter's diary and improves it; goes shopping with Mom and tries to make her buy him some really nice new sneakers; is horrified when his old enemy Bossy Bill turns up at school; and tries by any means, to win the class soccer match.

About the Author

Photo: Francesco Guidicini

Francesca Simon spent her childhood on the beach in California and then went to Yale and Oxford Universities to study medieval history and literature. She now lives in London with her family. She has written over forty-five books and won the Children's Book of the Year in 2008 at the Galaxy British Book Awards for *Horrid Henry and the Abominable Snowman*.